Enduro and Other
EXTREME MOUNTAIN BIKING

by Elliott Smith

Consultant: Daniel Lee
Outdoor Emergency Care Certified

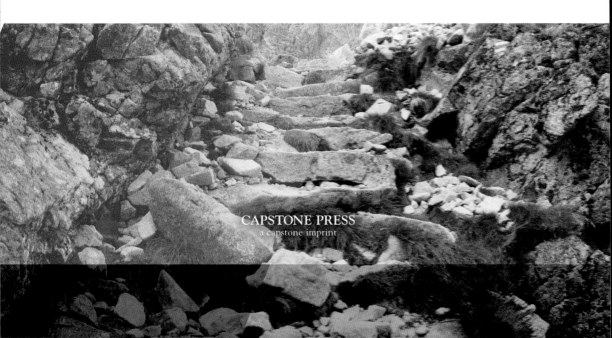

CAPSTONE PRESS
a capstone imprint

Edge Books are published by Capstone Press
1710 Roe Crest Drive
North Mankato, Minnesota 56003
www.capstonepub.com

Library of Congress Cataloging-in-Publication Data
Names: Smith, Elliott, 1976- author.
Title: Enduro and other extreme mountain biking / By Elliott
Smith.
Description: North Mankato, Minnesota : Edge Books, An imprint
of Capstone Press, [2020] | Series: Natural thrills | Audience: Age
8-9. | Audience: Grade 4 to 6.
Identifiers: LCCN 2019008690| ISBN 9781543573244 (hardcover) |
ISBN 9781543573305 (ebook pdf)
Subjects: LCSH: Motocross—Juvenile literature. | Mountain
biking—Juvenile literature. | Extreme sports—Juvenile literature.
Classification: LCC GV1060.12 .S65 2020 | DDC 796.7/56—dc23
LC record available at https://lccn.loc.gov/2019008690

Editorial Credits
Anna Butzer, editor; Cynthia Della-Rovere, designer;
Kelly Garvin, media researcher; Katy LaVigne, production specialist

Photo Credits
Alamy: Actionplus/Action Plus Sports Images, 5, Bill Freeman, 21, Buzz Pictures, 27, Cameron Cormack, 13, Chris
Strickland, 9, Ironstring, 7, NicVW, 14, Scott Markewitz/Cavan Images, 23, sportpoint, 19, Tony LeMoignan, 11;
Shutterstock: bochimsang12, 10 (top), Maciej Kopaniecki, 17, Mihail Fedoreenko, 25, MikeDotta, 29, NUTTANART
KHAMLAKSANA, 10 (bottom), Taras Hipp, cover, back cover

Design elements: Shutterstock: carlos castilla, Michal Rosenstein, pupsy

All internet sites appearing in back matter were available and accurate when this book was sent to press.

Table of Contents

CHAPTER 1

Race to the Finish

A rain-soaked Sam Hill stood at the start of the downhill race track in Champéry, Switzerland. The course was slick with mud, but Hill wasn't worried. The mountain biker wasn't going to let the conditions stop him from going fast. Even without the rain and hail, the course was one of the steepest, most dangerous courses in World Cup history. But Hill was ready for the challenge. Thirty riders went before him, each carefully taking on the mud-coated course. When Hill took his turn, though, there was no hesitation. His ride down the mountain earned him a third-place finish and the respect of his fellow racers. Hill became legendary in the mountain biking community because he pushed the limits.

> "I'm loving the enduro stuff," said Hill. "Anything you do in life, you set a goal and to achieve it, it's pretty special."

That downhill race was just the start for the Australian biker. He switched to enduro racing a few years later and immediately made an impression on the scene. Hill became one of the first riders to successfully use flat bike pedals. Most competitors clip their shoes to the pedals for a tighter grip. But Hill won back-to-back Enduro World Series championships using flat pedals. He has helped the sport reach new heights. His unique style and blinding speed has made him a fan favorite.

CHAPTER 2

What is Enduro?

There are many different styles of mountain biking. Enduro is one that's growing rapidly in popularity. Enduro requires riders to find a way up a mountain and race down to win. Enduro, also sometimes called "all-mountain," was inspired by rally car races, and the first competitions were held in the 1990s.

Enduro races are usually made up of three to six timed **stages** over one or two days. The timed stages are downhill and can feature steep drops and natural **obstacles**. Riders have specific times to clear for each stage. Going uphill, athletes either ride or hike with their bikes. Fortunately, the uphill sections of the race are not timed. The times from the downhill sections are then added up to determine the winner.

Oftentimes, enduro athletes must compete a course without any practice runs. This is called blind racing.

stage—a period or step in a process or activity
obstacle—an object or barrier that competitors must avoid during a race

You can't use just any bike for enduro racing. Riders need a strong bike with big, stiff wheels to help handle the rough **terrain** and jumps. Enduro bikes also have more **suspension** to help with control. Because of these features, athletes can go faster and quickly recover from any mistakes. During races, riders must use the same bike for each run. The racers need a combination of riding skills and excellent fitness to be able to ride up and down the hills. Some races can last nearly an hour.

suspension—the system of devices, like springs, supporting the upper part of a vehicle
terrain—the physical features of a piece of land

Enduro races can take place anywhere, but the courses are usually in areas with mountains or hills. This means steep inclines!

The best racers participate in the exclusive Enduro World Series, which features competitions around the globe. Some races, including Colorado's Keystone BME and California's Kamikaze Bike Games, feature divisions for young riders.

Visual Glossary

spare tube
Having a spare inner tube can keep a rider in the race. Enduro courses can be rough, and a flat tire could happen any time!

multi-use tool
This tool allows riders to adjust handlebars, tighten spokes, and even fix the chain if it breaks.

helmet
Some enduro riders bring two helmets for one race: one with a full-face mask and one without. A full-face mask gives a rider extra protection.

goggles
Goggles protect a rider's eyes from wind, dirt, water, and mud.

gloves
Gloves protect an athlete's hands. They also keep hands warm and help the rider grip handlebars.

enduro bike
An enduro bike has extra suspension. This means the rider will experience less impact on rough trails and terrain.

CHAPTER 3

Downhill

Speed is the name of the game in downhill racing. The only goal is to get to the bottom of the mountain as fast as possible, but it isn't that easy. One small mistake during a run can cost valuable seconds.

Learning the course is key for downhill athletes. They make multiple runs down the course. Each time they make adjustments to get down the hill faster. They are looking for the perfect path to victory.

strategy—a careful plan or method

The path to victory can be full of sharp turns, big drops, and rough landings!

Downhill runs last anywhere from three to five minutes. Courses are set up with a strip of tape on each side. Riders must remain within the tape identifying the course. Racers often must choose what **strategy** they want to use to get down the fastest. There may be a small jump with a safe landing that covers less ground. Another path may present a huge jump with a difficult landing. Or there may be a jump-free path that could take longer to race. Make the right choice and a rider could be headed for victory.

Downhill riders stay low to help increase their speed.

Downhill bikes are specially designed to ride in one direction—down. Their low center of gravity helps increase speed. Because these bikes are low, they remain **stable** and are easier to handle on rough courses. They also have large, spiked tires that can ride over rough terrain without going flat. Many pros change tires and parts after practice runs to make their bikes faster.

Downhill racing got started in the 1970s. A group of friends began racing down a dirt **fire road** in California named Repack. Before long, more bikers started arriving at the races, and the event became a success. Now, downhill racing is popular around the world. Some ski areas are turned into downhill bike courses during summer months. The Downhill World Cup is the biggest event on the bike racing calendar every year.

stable—not easily moved
fire road—a road built specifically for the purpose of access for fire management

CHAPTER 4

Cross Country

A marathon on two wheels, cross-country mountain biking puts a focus on long distances. While they don't experience big jumps or large obstacles, cross country riders must be great athletes. **Endurance** is key to success in cross country, or "XC." Most trails feature long periods of **ascending** and **descending** the mountain. Races can last hours, or even days, so physical fitness is important.

ascend—to move from a lower place to a higher place
descend—to move from a higher place to a lower place
endurance—the ability to withstand difficult activity

Cross country is the most common form of mountain bike racing, but it is not the easiest. The trails vary in size, shape, and distance, and riders must maintain bike control in difficult conditions. Athletes usually start races all at the same time. At the beginning of some races, more than 100 competitors fight for the top position.

During cross-country races, speed and climbing are important elements. Athletes must use several skills to make ascending less difficult. Riders need to stay seated and keep a steady pedaling motion.

Cross-country races take place on many different kinds of terrain.

One skill riders need in XC racing is the ability to climb the mountain quickly. The best riders often move ahead of the pack during these uphill sections. In order to do that, they must have the correct bike and firm tires. A good cross-country bike is very light, many are less than 25 pounds (11 kilograms). Compare that to a downhill bike, which is nearly 8 pounds (4 kg) heavier. Most cross-country bikes have front suspension and longer **wheelbases** to put riders into better climbing positions.

Cross country is the mountain biking style that is easiest for beginners to learn. Most mountains have bike trails, and riders are eager to push themselves in this fun racing style.

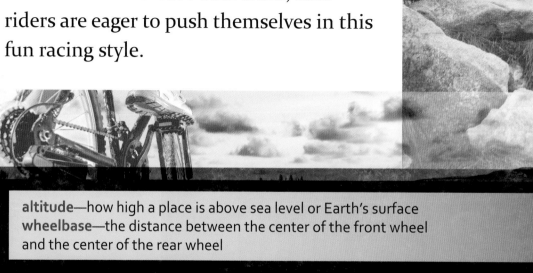

altitude—how high a place is above sea level or Earth's surface
wheelbase—the distance between the center of the front wheel and the center of the rear wheel

Cross-country cycling might be the easiest to learn, but that doesn't mean it is easy! A rider must be in good physical shape.

Cross-Country Marathon

While most XC races are 5 to 25 miles (8 to 40 kilometers), there are several that are much longer. Cross-country marathon races range anywhere from 37 to 100 miles (60 to 161 km). Other races feature a time element, ranging from 12 to 24 hours. Some races allow riders to work as a team, while other races are for solo riders.

One of the most well-known cross-country marathons is the Leadville Trail 100 Run. Bikers go across high-**altitude** trails in the Rocky Mountains for a scenic and challenging ride. The race forces riders to climb to more than 12,000 feet (3,650 m) above sea level. The race is so popular that the event has a yearly lottery to enter. More than 1,500 riders take part each year.

CHAPTER 5

Dirt Jumping and Slopestyle

Catching big air is the plan in dirt jumping, a mountain bike style that concentrates on amazing tricks. Where another biker might just see a large mound, a dirt jumper sees opportunity. Dirt jumpers use natural sections of dirt or build ramps to create an **aerial** playground.

aerial—relating to, or occurring in the air or atmosphere

Extreme mountain bike champion
Brian Lopes is an expert dirt jumper.

Ramps and mounds of varying heights are scattered on the course. Riders then approach the jumps, trying to get the most possible height, or "air." Building up speed helps riders perform a variety of tricks before landing. Having a good flow for jumps and tricks is key for riders on a dirt-jumping course. Flow is when the turns, jumps, and obstacles on the course work together to create an ideal ride.

While some dirt-jumping locations are found within bike trails, others have been created. Groups of riders, using shovels and other hand tools, move dirt and create jumps. The process can take weeks because the dirt must settle and harden. With an adult's help, even beginner riders can make a small set of jumps in a backyard.

Slopestyle is closely related to dirt jumping. Many of the tricks, which happen in mid-air, have unique names. A Can-Can is a move in which a rider takes one foot off the pedal and swings it over the bike. In a tailwhip, the rider kicks the back end of the bike in a rotation around the handlebars. The Superman leaves bikers soaring through the air while holding on to the end of the seat.

An experienced slopestyle rider performs the Superman.

Dirt jumping can be very dangerous. Riders practice their tricks on a much smaller level before taking them to competitions. Tricks are easier to perform with a lightweight bike. Front brakes are removed on a dirt jump bike to make the bike lighter. Slopestyle bikes are a little heavier and firmer to help absorb landing big jumps. They also have shocks to help with tough landings.

CHAPTER 6

Freeriding

Some bikers just want to ride without worrying about rules or guidelines. The excitement of going down a mountain any way possible is what inspires freeriding. Freeriding means riding without a set course, goals, or rules in natural terrain. Riders use their own creativity and skill to get down the mountain. Freeriders share traits with downhill bikers and dirt jumpers, and most riders are skilled in all three styles.

The Red Bull Rampage

One of the most unique freeride competitions is the annual Red Bull Rampage. This extremely tough race is special because the course is not set up in advance for the riders. When racers arrive at the site, they are responsible for digging and building a path down the mountain. That usually means no two racers ride the same way down.

Teams use pickaxes, shovels, and other materials to create the bumps, jumps, and paths needed to race. Because this competition is so challenging, only the best riders get approved to race. This results in some breathtaking performances. Canadian biker Brett Rheeder won the 2018 Red Bull Rampage, held in Utah, thanks to a 360-degree jump and backflips!

Freeriding is mostly about creativity and skill.

Freeriding competitions are less about speed and more about imagination. It is up to the rider to determine the most creative way down the trail. A rider may decide to use a fallen log as part of a run. Another may perform a series of tricks or jumps. The inventiveness is what attracts athletes to freeriding. Freeride bikes are lightweight in order to give riders the ability to **maneuver** tricky trails. They have strong suspensions to absorb drops. Unlike downhill bikes, freeride bikes are built to help riders go up a mountain.

maneuver—a planned and controlled movement that requires practiced skills

CHAPTER 7

How to Get Started

Enduro and other extreme mountain biking sports offer big thrills and plenty of fun. But it takes more than a bike to get started. The proper safety equipment is a must for the sport. A helmet is a necessity for any bike ride, but mountain biking may require a specialized helmet. Full-face helmets with removable chin bars provide more safety. An adult should be present during rides to help with any issues.

Selecting the right bike is also important. Before buying, go to a bike store and try several options. Finding a bike with a solid frame is key. Other parts can be upgraded as a rider improves their skills.

Young riders should get comfortable with the attack position on their bikes. That is the basic position and the first technique to be mastered before beginning off-road riding. The attack position has a rider stand with the pedals level, elbows bent, and their weight centered over the bike. A rider's grip on the handlebars should be loose. This allows the bike to move freely.

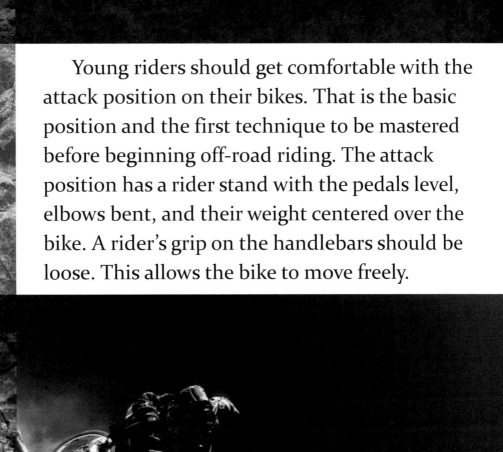

Many communities offer programs for young riders. But using bikes to explore a neighborhood is a great place to start. Some biking areas also feature pump tracks. These are small, looping trails that riders can go around nonstop without pedaling. They often feature small bumps and jumps that are perfect for beginner bikers. Simple tricks like jumping the curb or riding down a single step are great ways to practice.

When the opportunity to try mountain biking comes along, start small. Find a moderate trail to ride with experienced bikers and an adult. Stay close to other riders and listen to their instructions. Don't hesitate to hop off the bike and walk during difficult sections. Mastering all the cool moves in mountain biking takes years of practice. Getting outside and learning how to ride is a great first step.

Mountain biking is a great way to stay active, make new friends, and enjoy the outdoors!

GLOSSARY

aerial (AYR-ee-uhl)—relating to, or occurring in the air or atmosphere

altitude (AL-ti-tood)—how high a place is above sea level or Earth's surface

ascend (uh-SEND)—to move from a lower place to a higher place

descend (dee-SEND)—to move from a higher place to a lower place

endurance (en-DUR-enss)—the ability to withstand difficult activity

fire road (FYR ROHD)—a road built specifically for the purpose of access for fire management

maneuver (muh-NOO-ver)—a planned and controlled movement that requires practiced skills

obstacle (OB-stuh-kuhl)—an object or barrier that competitors must avoid during a race

stable (STAY-buhl)—not easily moved

stage (STAYJ)—a period or step in a process or activity

strategy (STRAT-uh-jee)—a careful plan or method

suspension (suh-SPEN-shuhn)—the system of devices, like springs, supporting the upper part of a vehicle

terrain (tuh-RAYN)—the physical features of a piece of land

wheelbase (WEEL-bayss)—the distance between the center of the front wheel and the center of the rear wheel

READ MORE

Abdo, Kenny. *Mountain Bikes*. Off Road Vehicles. Minneapolis, MN: Abdo Zoom, 2017.

Nagle, Jeanne. *Extreme Biking.* Sports to the Extreme. New York: Rosen Publishing, 2015.

Whiting, Jim. *Mountain Biking.* Odysseys in Extreme Sports. Mankato, MN: Creative Education, 2018.

INTERNET SITES

International Mountain Biking Association: For Youth
https://www.imba.com/ride/for-youth

Mountain Biking for Kids
https://mtbwithkids.com/

Red Bull: Mountain Biking
https://www.redbull.com/us-en/tags/mtb

INDEX